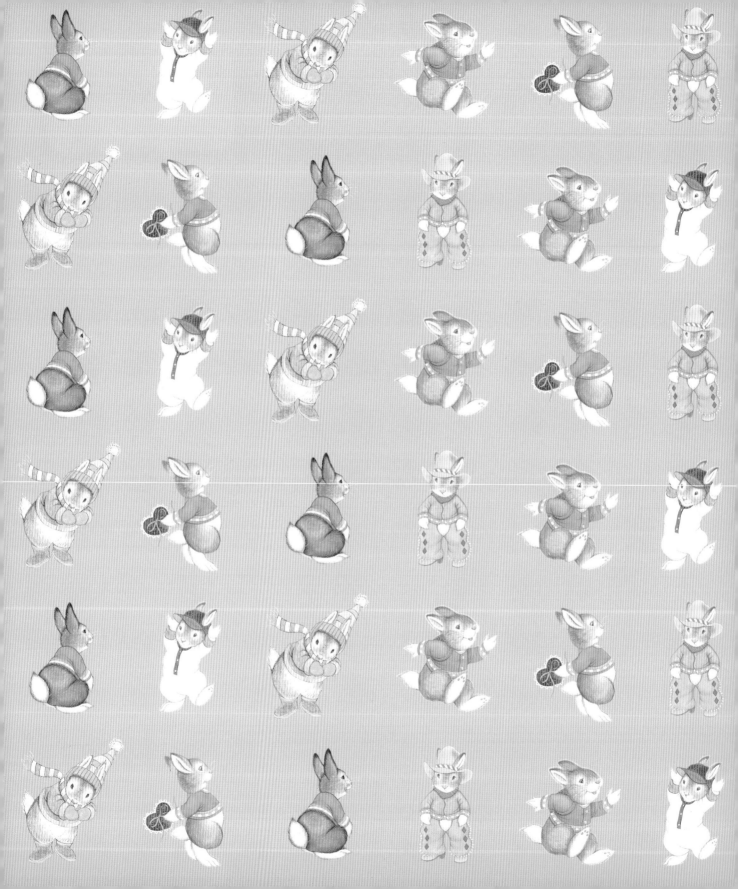

波波唸翻天系列 6

波波 郊遊去

Justine Korman 著

Lucinda McQueen 繪

柯美玲 譯

三民書局

For Ron, who makes every trip exciting
—J.K.

獻給朗恩，因為他，每一次出遊都好玩極了
—J.K.

For Justine, storyteller extraordinaire,
with countless bunny thanks
—Lucinda

獻給賈斯汀，一流的說故事高手，獻上數不盡的兔子謝謝
— 露辛達

The sun was **shining** brightly the morning of the kinderbunny class field **trip**. Ten excited kinderbunnies hippety-hopped in front of Easter Bunny Elementary School.

Everyone was smiling—except, of course, the grumpy bunny. This year Hopper was leading the field trip for the first time.

幼幼班舉辦郊遊的那天早上，陽光非常燦爛。十隻興高采烈的小兔子在復活節兔寶寶小學前面蹦蹦跳跳。

每隻小兔子都在微笑——只有這隻愛抱怨的兔子例外。今年是波波頭一回負責帶隊出去郊遊。

"What if I lose a bunny?" Hopper worried. "What if some bunny gets sick on the bus?"

He tried to **count** the kinderbunnies as they **bounced** here, there, and everywhere. "One bunny, two bunnies, three bunnies, four...now I need to find six more," the grumpy bunny **grumbled**.

「萬一有小兔子不見了，怎麼辦？」波波好擔心。「萬一有小兔子在巴士上不舒服，怎麼辦？」

他試著數那些這裡蹦蹦、那裡跳跳，到處亂跑的小兔子。「一隻小兔子、二隻小兔子、三隻小兔子、四隻……現在還得去找那另外六隻小兔子。」這隻愛抱怨的兔子嘟嚷著。

3

At last, Hopper had all
ten kinderbunnies
counted.

1, 2, 3, 4, 5, 6, 7, 8, 9, 10

bunnies **climbed** the steep **stairs** of the bus.

最後，波波終於數完了十隻小兔子。一、二、三、四、五、六、七、八、九、十——小兔子們一一爬上了巴士陡陡的階梯。

Hopper had hoped the kinderbunnies would sit still, but they were much too excited. In fact, some of the bunnies bounced right off their bus seats!

波波好希望小兔子們能坐著不要動。可是他們太興奮了。事實上，有好幾隻小兔子已經從他們的坐椅上跳了起來！

The bus ride to the big city was a teacher's **nightmare**. Hopper
tried to **calm** the riot. But the minute he got one kinderbunny **settled
down**, nine more needed his attention. The grumpy bunny was so
distracted, he could **barely** keep his eyes on the road.

在巴士開往大城市的路上，簡直就是一個老師的惡夢。

波波試著平息騷動，但是他才讓一隻小兔子平靜下來，卻又得注意其他九隻。這隻愛抱怨的兔子心煩意亂，幾乎無法專心看路。

Hopper wasn't the only one who wanted the bus trip to end. Peter couldn't wait to see the dinobunnies. He **tugged** at Hopper's sleeve. "Are we there yet?"

The grumpy bunny **rolled** his eyes. "We haven't gone a mile since the last time you asked!"

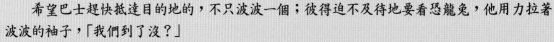
希望巴士趕快抵達目的地的，不只波波一個；彼得迫不及待地要看恐龍兔，他用力拉著波波的袖子，「我們到了沒？」
愛抱怨的兔子轉了轉眼睛，「從你上次問我到現在，還走不到一哩路呢！」

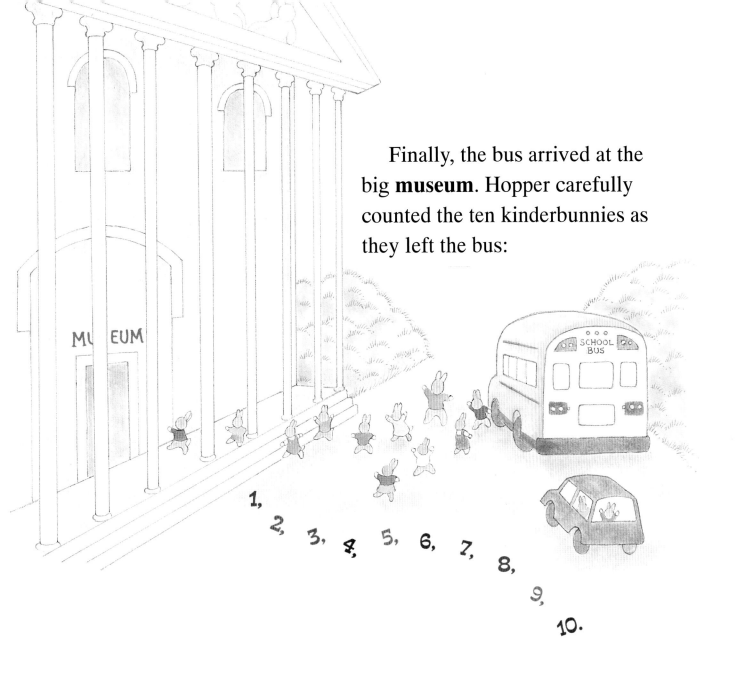

Finally, the bus arrived at the big **museum**. Hopper carefully counted the ten kinderbunnies as they left the bus:

1, 2, 3, 4, 5, 6, 7, 8, 9, 10.

最後，巴士終於抵達大博物館了。十隻小兔子一隻一隻下車，波波則是小心地數著：一、二、三、四、五、六、七、八、九、十。

Then he counted them again inside the huge museum. Peter's voice **echoed** through the great hall. "Are we there yet?"

Hopper sighed. "Yes, we are. Now, I want everyone to listen up! Remember the most important rule: Stay together! I don't want any of you **wandering** off."

The kinderbunnies **nodded**. "We promise," they said.

然後，在巨大的博物館裡，他又數了一遍。彼得的聲音迴盪在寬敞的大廳裡，「我們到了沒？」

波波嘆了一口氣，「是的，我們到了。現在，我要大家注意聽！記得最重要的規定是：要團體行動！我可不想你們任何一個走丟了。」小兔子們點點頭說，「我們保證。」

"All right. Let's start with the **prehistoric** rabbits," Hopper decided.
Peter **cheered**. "Yea! Yea!"
"Sshhh!" Hopper **hissed**. "A museum is a place for quiet." He led the
bunnies through the **arch** labeled BUNNIES OLD.

「好！我們就從史前兔子開始。」波波做了這樣的決定。

「耶！耶！」彼得叫好。

「噓！」波波噓了一聲。「博物館是個安靜的地方。」他帶小兔子們穿過標示著「古代兔子」的拱門。

Suddenly, a huge **skeleton** towered above them! "Bunnysaurus Rex!" Peter whispered in **awe**.

Hopper's **jaw** dropped. "That creature looks wilder than a kinderbunny!" he said to himself.

Hopper showed his class the bones of other **critters** who lived long ago.

"Amazing! I wish we could stay for a week!" Peter **squealed**.

"I know," Hopper agreed. "But there's so much more to see. Let's move on!"

Peter did not hear Hopper. He was too busy pretending to be a Bunnysaurus Rex.

忽然，一塊巨大的骸骨出現在他們頭上！「雷克斯暴龍兔吔！」彼得以充滿敬畏的口吻低聲地說。波波的下巴掉了下來。「這動物看起來比小兔子還野蠻。」他自言自語。

波波又帶著學生參觀其他歷史更久遠的動物骸骨。
「太驚人了！真希望我們能在這裡待上一個星期。」彼得歡呼著。
「我知道，」波波也有同感。「可是要看的東西還很多，大家繼續往前走！」
彼得並沒有聽見波波說的話，他忙著假裝自己是一隻雷克斯暴龍兔。

13

Next, the kinderbunnies went through the arch marked BUNNIES BOLD. There they saw shining suits of **armor**, bright **banners**, and sharp **swords**.

"This is how bunnies **fought** their battles in the Middle Ages," Hopper explained.

接著，這群小兔子走過一個寫著「兔子勇士」的拱門。在那裡，他們看到一套一套閃閃發亮的盔甲、鮮艷的旗幟，還有銳利的刀劍。「中古世紀的兔子就是這樣在戰場上打仗。」波波做如此的說明。

Daisy and Flopsy were not listening. They were fighting their own battle—over Flopsy's lunch!

The two battling bunnies were left behind when the class moved on to BUNNIES LIVING IN THE COLD.

小兔寶寶黛絲和晃晃並沒有注意聽，他們自己也忙著打仗──爭奪晃晃的午餐！
當全班繼續往「寒帶兔子館」前進的時候，這兩隻打著仗的小兔子落在隊伍的後面。

"Brrr!" Hopper **shivered**. Just looking at the snowy scenes in the glass cases gave him the **chills**.

"These bunnies build their homes out of ice and snow," he told the group.

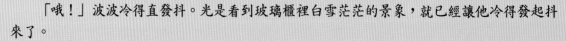

「哦！」波波冷得直發抖。光是看到玻璃櫃裡白雪茫茫的景象，就已經讓他冷得發起抖來了。

「這些兔子用冰和雪蓋房子。」他告訴那些小兔子。

"I wonder what it would be like to be an Eskibunny," **mused** a dreamy bunny named Dean. He pictured building his very own ice **castle** and riding a pet **seal** named Sam.

Dean was far away when Hopper said, "Time for lunch. Follow me!"

「真不曉得當愛斯基摩兔是什麼滋味，」一隻愛做夢的小兔子狄恩沈思著。他想像自己蓋了一座冰城堡，還騎著一隻名叫山姆的寵物海豹。當波波說「午餐時間到了，跟我來！」的時候，狄恩已經落後大家好遠了。

The bunnies got out their brown bags. They brought milk and juice—and carrot cake, of course. And they did their usual amount of **spilling**. While Hopper **mopped** up, Bingo climbed into the fountain. The class **clown** couldn't **resist striking** a funny pose!

In fact, Bingo was having so much fun posing, he didn't see the class move on to the Hall of Art.

小兔子們拿出自己的褐色紙袋，他們帶了牛奶和果汁——當然，還有紅蘿蔔蛋糕。和平常一樣，他們還是把食物灑得到處都是。就在波波東擦西擦的時候，小兔寶寶賓果爬進噴泉裡。這個班上的小丑忍不住擺了一個可笑的姿勢！

事實上，賓果還有很多可笑的姿勢要擺，根本沒看到他們班已經往藝術廳走去了。

小兔子們在偉大的藝術作品前面追來追去,波波氣得在後面追。「等一下!」他上氣不接下氣地喊著,「你們……錯過……欣賞藝術的機會了!」

The kinderbunnies **chased** each other past great **masterpieces**. Hopper huffed and puffed behind them. "Wait!" he panted. "You're... missing the...art!"

But one bunny wasn't missing anything. Arthur decided to stay and **sketch** what he saw.

但是，有一隻小兔子甚麼也沒錯過。亞瑟決定留在那裡，把他看到的東西畫下來。

"That's the last stop on our tour," Hopper said. "**Line up** for the bus, please."

Then he counted: "One, two, three, four...there must be six bunnies more!" The grumpy bunny pulled his ears in **distress**. Where were the other bunnies?

"Oh, no!" Hopper **wailed**. He wanted to turn the museum upside down to search for his students. "But I'm only one bunny!" he said in **despair**.

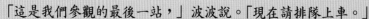

「這是我們參觀的最後一站，」波波說。「現在請排隊上車。」

　　然後他就數著：「一、二、三、四……應該還有六隻小兔子啊！」這隻愛抱怨的兔子苦惱地拉著耳朵。其他的小兔子在哪裡呢？「哦，不！」波波難過地叫出聲來。他好想把整個博物館掀起來找他的學生。「可是我只是隻兔子啊！」他絕望地說。

Suddenly, Hopper remembered something his teacher had taught him a long time ago: Think first.

So Hopper sat down and thought.

突然，波波想起很久很久以前老師教過他的：先想一想。
於是波波就坐下來想一想。

他想著剛剛小兔子們在博物館裡參觀的每一個地方，試著回想每一隻小兔子到過哪裡。
「我想到了！」波波跳了起來。「我要順著原來的路回去找。」

He thought about each place the bunnies had visited in the museum. He tried to remember where each kinderbunny had been. "I've got it!" Hopper jumped to his feet. "I'll **retrace** our steps."

Just then the lost bunnies came running to join the group.

"We heard you say, 'Oh, no!'" Peter **exclaimed**. "Is something wrong?"

就在這個時候，走失的小兔子們統統跑回隊伍來了。
「我們聽到你說，『哦，不！』」彼得大聲地說。「發生了甚麼事啊？」

Hopper counted his kinderbunnies one through ten and sighed with **relief**. "Not anymore! Let's go home before anything else can happen."

Quickly Hopper helped the bunnies back on the bus.

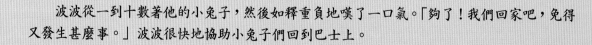

波波從一到十數著他的小兔子，然後如釋重負地嘆了一口氣。「夠了！我們回家吧，免得又發生甚麼事。」波波很快地協助小兔子們回到巴士上。

Then he **sank** gratefully into his seat. "What a field trip! This has to be my worst day ever!" the grumpy bunny **muttered**. "The minute we get back, I'm telling Sir Byron, 'No more field trips for this teacher— never, ever!' I'll put my **paw** down!"

他感激地癱坐在位子上。「好個郊遊！長這麼大，從來沒有像今天這麼慘過！」這隻愛抱怨的兔子低聲埋怨著。「待會兒一回去，我馬上就要告訴拜倫先生，『下次別再找我帶隊郊遊了——下不為例！』我會很堅定地拒絕的！」

But a strange thing happened when the bus reached the school.
Hopper found himself **surrounded** by happy kinderbunnies.
"This was the best field trip ever!" Peter **declared**.

　　但是，當巴士回到學校的時候，一件奇怪的事情發生了。波波發現一隻隻開心的小兔子
圍著他。「這是最棒的一次郊遊！」彼得叫了起來。

"It was the most fun I've ever had!" Daisy cried.
"No, it was the most fun *I've* ever had!" Flopsy shouted.
And the battling bunnies were at it again, until Sir Byron **appeared**.

「我從來沒有玩得這麼開心過！」黛絲大聲地說。
「才不是咧，應該是我玩得最開心才對！」晃晃大叫。
兩隻小兔子又打鬧了起來，直到拜倫先生出現。

The Great Hare **clapped** Hopper on the back and said, "Good job. I'm **counting on** you to lead the trip again next year."

The grumpy bunny thought about saying no. Then he looked at the **giggling** kinderbunnies and couldn't remember what he'd been so grumpy about. In fact, Hopper turned to Sir Byron and asked, "Do we have to wait a whole year?"

*The best part about traveling
is when the trip is done:
Your eyes are filled with new sights,
and your heart is filled with fun!*

兔老爹拍拍波波的背說,「做得很好。明年郊遊領隊的事就靠你了。」這隻愛抱怨的兔子原本想拒絕。但是當他看著那些咯咯笑的小兔子時,也就不記得自己剛剛在埋怨些甚麼了。事實上,波波轉過身來問拜倫先生說,「我們還得再等一整年嗎?」

旅行最好玩的部分是當旅程結束時:
你的雙眼滿載著新的風景,你的心中充滿了快樂!

chill [tʃɪl] 名 冷顫
clap [klæp] 動 拍
climb [klaɪm] 動 爬
clown [klaʊn] 名 小丑
count [kaʊnt] 動 數
count on　依靠
critter [`krɪtɚ] 名 動物

appear [ə`pɪr] 動 出現
arch [ɑrtʃ] 名 拱門
armor [`ɑrmɚ] 名 盔甲
awe [ɔ] 名 敬畏

banner [`bænɚ] 名 旗幟
barely [`bɛrlɪ] 副 幾乎不
bounce [baʊns] 動 跳起

declare [dɪ`klɛr] 動 宣告
despair [dɪ`spɛr] 名 絕望
distracted [dɪ`stræktɪd] 形 心煩意亂的
distress [dɪ`strɛs] 名 苦惱

calm [kɑm] 動 使平靜下來
castle [`kæsl̩] 名 城堡
chase [tʃes] 動 追
cheer [tʃɪr] 動 喝采

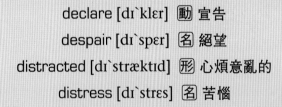

echo [`ɛko] 動 發出回音
exclaim [ɪk`sklem] 動 喊叫

F

fight [faɪt] 動 戰鬥（過去式 fought）

G

giggle [ˋgɪgḷ] 動 咯咯地笑

grumble [ˋgrʌmbḷ] 動 發牢騷

H

hiss [hɪs] 動 發出噓聲

J

jaw [dʒɔ] 名 下巴

L

line up 排隊 《for》

M

masterpiece [ˋmæstɚˏpis] 名 名作

mop [mɑp] 動 擦去 《up》

muse [mjuz] 動 沈思

museum [mjuˋziəm] 名 博物館

mutter [ˋmʌtɚ] 動 抱怨

N

nightmare [ˋnaɪtˏmɛr] 名 惡夢

nod [nɑd] 動 點頭

P

paw [pɔ] 名 腳掌

prehistoric [ˏpriɪsˋtɔrɪk] 形 史前的

R

relief [rɪˋlif] 名 寬慰

resist [rɪ`zɪst] 勔 忍住

retrace [rɪ`tres] 勔 沿（相同的路）走

roll [rol] 勔 轉動

seal [sil] 名 海豹

settle down　平靜下來

shine [ʃaɪn] 勔 閃耀

shiver [`ʃɪvɚ] 勔 發抖

sight [saɪt] 名 風景

sink [sɪŋk] 勔 癱倒 （過去式sank）

skeleton [`skɛlətn̩] 名 骸骨

sketch [skɛtʃ] 勔 素描

spill [spɪl] 勔 灑落

squeal [skwil] 勔 發出長而尖的歡呼

stairs [stɛrz] 名 樓梯

strike [straɪk] 勔 擺 （姿勢）

surround [sə`raund] 勔 圍繞

sword [sɔrd] 名 劍

trip [trɪp] 名 旅行

tug [tʌg] 勔 用力拉 《at》

wail [wel] 勔 悲哀地說

wander [`wɑndɚ] 勔 迷路 《off》

～ 看的繪本＋聽的繪本　童話小天地最能捉住孩子的心 ～

為孩子寫～彩色的夢

🌙 **兒童文學叢書**

·童話小天地·

○ **奇妙的紫貝殼**
簡　宛·文　朱美靜·圖

○ **九重葛笑了**
陳　冷·文　吳佩蓁·圖

○ **銀毛與斑斑**
李民安·文　廖健宏·圖

○ **屋頂上的祕密**
劉靜娟·文　郝洛玟·圖

○ **石頭不見了**
李民安·文　翱　子·圖

○ **奇奇的磁鐵鞋**
林黛嫚·文　黃子瑄·圖

○ **智慧市的糊塗市民**
劉靜娟·文　邰欣／倪靖·圖

○ **丁伶郎**
潘人木·文
鄭凱軍／羅小紅·圖

嗨～話弟選進好夢，在爸爸媽媽甜蜜的說故事時間就要開始囉！

國家圖書館出版品預行編目資料

波波郊遊去 / Justine Korman 著;Lucinda McQueen
繪;柯美玲譯.－－初版一刷.－－臺北市;三民,民
90
　　面;公分－－(探索英文叢書.波波唸翻天系列;6)
中英對照
ISBN 957－14－3445－0　(平裝)

　1.英國語言－讀本

805.18　　　　　　　　　　　　　　90003949

網路書店位址　http://www.sanmin.com.tw

© 波波郊遊去

著作人　Justine Korman
繪　圖　Lucinda McQueen
譯　者　柯美玲
發行人　劉振強
著作財
產權人　三民書局股份有限公司
　　　　臺北市復興北路三八六號
發行所　三民書局股份有限公司
　　　　地址 / 臺北市復興北路三八六號
　　　　電話 / 二五〇〇六六〇〇
　　　　郵撥 / 〇〇〇九九九八——五號
印刷所　三民書局股份有限公司
門市部　復北店 / 臺北市復興北路三八六號
　　　　重南店 / 臺北市重慶南路一段六十一號
初版一刷　中華民國九十年四月
編　號　S 85594
定　價　新臺幣壹佰捌拾元
行政院新聞局登記證局版臺業字第〇二〇〇號

ISBN　957－14－3445－0　(平裝)